I0557166

# The Adventures of King

Story by Ezra Turner

Illustrations by Ira Philip III

ISBN: 978-0-969833-22-2

Published by Print Link
Printed in Canada

# Dedication

*To my daughters, Renee and Nicole.*
*Many thanks to Miss Margo Smith, Mr. Stephen Notman,*
*Mr. Glen Shorto and Mr. Chris Watson,*
*and Dr. Nicole Harford.*

# Table of Contents

# Wolf-dog

The adventures of King took place in the early 1900s, near the majestic Rocky Mountains in the United States of America. King belonged to a discharged army sergeant, named Mr. Herbert, who lived all alone in a small cabin deep in the dark woods. The nearest town, called Fiddler's Town, with a population of only one hundred people, was just fifteen miles away.

When Mr. Herbert was discharged from the army, years before King was born, he took with him one of the army dogs he had named Lady. Lady and Mr. Herbert settled down very well together in their cosy cabin and, though there were just the two of them, they were never lonely.

In this part of the country, small packs of wolves often attacked the livestock. The leader of the wolves was a large ash-coloured wolf known as "Big Gray". Big Gray was fearless ... he even attacked men with rifles, leaving many wounded and scarred for life.

One night, Big Gray entered Mr. Herbert's pigpen. Loud squeals and Lady's steady growl woke Mr. Herbert out of his sleep. He grabbed his rifle and hurried out of the cabin. Luckily the moon was so bright he could see everything clearly. Among the pack of wolves Mr. Herbert recognized Big Gray carrying away one of the small pigs in his jaws, leaving the other three wolves to fend for themselves. Mr. Herbert shouted at the wolves and they stopped attacking the pigs and slowly moved towards him. Sensing danger, Lady raced straight at the wolves and attacked with such fierceness, they ran for their lives.

The following evening, while Mr. Herbert was enjoying a cup of coffee, he heard a howl outside. It was no ordinary howl, but one filled with vengeance. He looked out of the window, and there stood Big Gray, looking bigger than ever. Lady jumped through the open window and leaped on Big Gray. Mr. Herbert grabbed his gun but couldn't fire a single shot, because he didn't want to take the chance of shooting Lady. The fierce fight lasted for at least five minutes. Exhausted, the dog and the wolf suddenly stopped fighting and looked into each other's eyes, both animals weak from the long battle.

Big Gray turned and walked slowly away. Lady looked at Mr. Herbert for a long moment and then ran to Big Gray. They rubbed noses, wagged their tails, and ran off together into the woods. Mr. Herbert could not believe what he was seeing. He yelled out, "Lady, come back! Don't leave me!" But with a flash of her tail she was gone and he was left all alone. Mr. Herbert put his head in his hands and wept as though his heart would break.

One stormy night, a whole year later, while Mr. Herbert was in his cabin in front of a blazing fire, he heard a howl so loud it sent a shiver down his spine. He looked out the window and saw something moving steadily closer to his door through the rain. It was Lady! She carried something gently with her mouth and dropped it carefully outside the door, quickly turned and ran back into the deep woods. Mr. Herbert threw open the door and there on the doorstep lay a tiny puppy. He carried it gently indoors, safely cradled in his big rough hands, then dried the little creature carefully and set him down close to the fire.

Slowly a warm feeling spread all over Mr. Herbert – a special joy had entered his life again. As the days passed, Mr. Herbert spent his time training the puppy, but he could not decide on a name. He noticed that the puppy was always eager to learn and caught on quickly too, as if he had done everything before. He even walked around the cabin like he was royalty. One day while the puppy was strutting around, Mr. Herbert smiled and said, "King! Yes, I will call you King." The puppy ran to him and heeled, just as he had been taught. Mr. Herbert stroked his silky coat, pulled him closer and laughed with joy. During the days that followed, King spent most of his time either with Mr. Herbert or roaming the forest.

One afternoon as King was wandering through the woods, he came upon two cougar cubs playing. He sat down and stared in fascination for a while, watching until he couldn't resist the temptation any longer. Then he leaped up and joined in the fun. The cubs were wary and were about to run, but then somehow they realized that King posed no danger to them. Without much thought, they returned to their play. King soon grew accustomed to their scratching and biting. He learned that he had to be swift to avoid getting hurt. The playing went on for hours, until they heard a loud hiss. King did not want to investigate that noise, so he returned to the cabin just in time for his supper. The game between the young dog and the cougar cubs went on for months. During their games, King learned the swift movements of the little cougar cubs and their clever tactics in capturing their prey with one swift, powerful motion.

As the days went by, King's body broadened and his teeth became as sharp as razors. Mr. Herbert often rebuked him saying, "King, you're coming home far too late at night." King knew he wasn't cross though, for he spoke with a smile. Mr.Herbert had learned to trust King's instincts and knew that King needed the adventure he was sure the woods provided. Next to his well, Mr.

Herbert built a wooden post with a bell on it, so that he could ring it whenever he wanted King to come home.

# The Bear Cub

One day while Mr. Herbert was in his cornfield, he heard loud howls and cries from an animal obviously in great pain. Picking up his rifle, he ran in the direction of the sounds. Nearby on the rocky path, he saw two wolves attacking a bear cub. Mr. Herbert fired a shot up in the air, and the wolves ran off, leaving the cub lying there. When Mr. Herbert reached the cub, he saw it had several nasty bites. He carried the cub to the cabin, where he gently cleaned the wounds as best he could. By evening the little cub had made himself comfortable in front of Mr. Herbert's fire. When King arrived home he scratched at the door. Mr. Herbert opened it, but when the cub saw the wolf dog he growled. King walked over to the furry creature and smacked him to the ground with a paw. The little cub turned on his back and submitted to King, who licked the baby bear's wounds until they were really clean. When King walked to the fireplace and lay down, the cub went too and lay down close to him, safe and content.

The next day the rooster's crowing awakened Mr. Herbert who was surprised to see that the little cub was happily curled up so close to King. In just a week, the little bear was running around again full of energy, his wounds beginning to heal. The cub had become very attached to King, who sometimes took him into the forest where they played together throughout the day.

One day while King and the cub were in the woods, Mr. Herbert was finishing his daily chores and having a drink of water from the well, when suddenly there was a loud growl. He turned to see a huge bear running straight at him. Her top lip was curled back and her fangs were showing, so Mr. Herbert knew the bear was not coming for a drink of water. He dropped his cup and raced toward the cabin with the bear following close on his heels. He did manage to reach the cabin, but before he could close the door, the bear pushed its massive weight against it and forced her way in. Mr. Herbert dodged around a table several times to avoid the bear's powerful claws, but then the bear knocked the table down with such force it shattered. The noise made the bear stop for a few seconds, just long enough for Mr. Herbert to get out of the cabin and slam the door behind him. He then ran as fast as he could to the wooden post and rang the bell for King. Meanwhile, the bear tore down the door and headed towards Mr. Herbert again, who quickly lowered himself into the well.

From his hiding place in the well, Mr. Herbert heard a fierce howl as King came running out of the woods. The bear turned around, flashing her fangs and swinging her mighty claws. King circled her cautiously and she turned to strike him, but he ran around to her opposite side. After a few minutes of twisting back and forth, the bear became tired of the 'game' and walked away. Then Mr. Herbert heard another cry. When he looked up he saw it was the cub. The huge bear's ears lifted at the sound and she ran toward the cub who was sitting there with a puzzled frown on its furry face. When the big bear reached the little one, the cub was so excited it ran around and around her, as they went happily off into the woods together.

# King To the Rescue

J ust a few miles outside of Fiddler's town, on a hillside surrounded by woods, a group of gypsies were camping. They had been there quite a few days. Their lively music and hectic dancing brought new life to the area and the town folks. Each day they could hear the music so clearly it sounded as if it were right outside their windows.

The gypsies had many little children who used to sing along with the older folks late into the night. Mark was one of the little boys; a mischievous thirteen year old, with long curly hair that hung way down his skinny frame. Mark sometimes ran away, to be found days later safe in the comfortable home of some country folks. He used to tell them all kinds of tales – like he had no family, or that a wild animal had chased him and he had barely managed to get away. But he told these tales so convincingly that folks would listen to him, and believe every word.

One night after their singing, when the gypsy children were put to bed – Mark felt the need for a new adventure. He waited quietly until everyone else was asleep then, in the still of the night, he crept out of the caravan and headed deeper into the forest. He was not afraid, because the gypsies believed the forest was their back garden and felt quite at home there. Mark had hidden in the forest and in its caves many times before. So this night was just like any other to him.

The next morning, when everyone was up and having breakfast, Mark could not be found. His mother and father were very concerned. Even though Mark had wandered off many times before, they still worried. His parents eventually gathered a search party together which split up into small groups to begin the search. Some went into the town. Others went deeper into the forest. The rest headed towards the mountains. However, at the end of the day, they all returned to their caravans without finding any trace of Mark. In fact they did not have a clue as to his whereabouts. That night was a sad one. No music or dancing, just the moaning of the wind.

The next day, everyone went out and searched afresh. Eventually, they came upon Mr. Herbert's cabin. He was busy working in his garden, when the gypsies greeted him. He looked them over and said with a smile, "May I help you?" One of them asked if he had seen a boy about thirteen years old but when Mr. Herbert said that he had not, Mark's father burst into tears. Mr. Herbert comforted the weeping man and said that if the boy was in the woods, he could find him. Mark's father stopped crying and said, "Oh please help us. Please."

Mr. Herbert walked over to the old bell and rang it once. The sound of the bell echoed all around, and a few minutes later King came running swiftly out of the forest. The gypsies huddled together in fear when they saw the size of the dog and the speed at which it moved towards them.

As the huge dog ran to his side and sat down, Mr. Herbert said, "Please don't be afraid of King." Then he asked for something that belonged to the boy and Mark's father pulled his son's cap out of his pocket. Mr. Herbert gave it to King to sniff, then said to the gypsies, "Follow King wherever he goes, have patience and trust in him. He is smarter than all of us put together." In a loud, firm voice he said,

"Go King! Go and find the boy!" King sniffed the cap one more time, turned and headed for the forest. Silence fell over the group. Mr. Herbert smiled encouragingly and pointed toward the trees, then the gypsies quickly set off, following King into the forest. The day was long and tiring. After the sun set the gypsies were happy to gather and sing their songs, while King sat on a flat rock and watched them, with a strange expression on his face.

The next day was cloudy and a heavy mist hung over the forest. The weather did not stop the search party though and King and his followers continued to hunt. Suddenly noisy yapping disturbed the peace of the forest. Everyone froze. King went to investigate the cry, and walking over to a large bush he was greeted by a wolf pup that was obviously very happy to see him. The pup jumped all over King, until he wrestled the pup to the ground, turned him on his back and exposed his belly. Then King turned and walked away, focussing on his search for Mark again. The gypsies followed, and to their surprise the young wolf tagged along behind them.

King was heading toward the mountains. Though they were only five miles away, it was such tough going, it felt more like twenty. The little wolf pup soon got up enough nerve to move up close behind King, all the time wagging his tail wildly. Suddenly the forest opened up into beautiful green pasture scattered with pretty white daisies.

Abruptly, the howls of a wolf pack echoed across the fields. The frightened gypsies stood still. King stood in front of them, his paws planted firmly in the lush grass, his ears up high, his chest puffed out as strong as steel. The gypsies, who only had knives, wondered if they should run back, but knew they would never make it up a tree to safety in time. They decided to stay back behind King with their knives ready. The wolves appeared one by one, silently circling the gypsies and King. It was the puppy who broke the silence and yapped loudly, trying to coax King on. Out of the pack walked a fierce looking wolf straight towards them. If the gypsies had seen this wolf under different circumstances, they would have sworn it was King. The two animals looked almost identical, but this wolf looked mean and was a little smaller than King.

King walked towards him until they were face to face in the center between the gypsies and the other wolves. Without flinching, the newcomer jumped at King, who dodged him with a circling movement, then gripped him by the throat and swung him around like a rag doll. Just as suddenly, he let the wolf go with a flinging motion so that it rolled over and over before it was able to get back up on its feet again. With its tail between its legs, the wolf slunk back to the pack.

Then a large ash-colored wolf appeared. The gypsies trembled when they saw the size of Big Gray. Even the other wolves shrank back with fear. Then the real battle began. Big Gray, despite all his experience and strength, was no match for King, and if it hadn't been for interference by Lady, King would have fought and killed his own father. When Lady jumped into the fray with them, they backed away from each other. Now that the fighting had stopped, the little pup went running up to Lady and began jumping excitedly around her before heading toward the trees. Then Lady and Big Gray followed the puppy back to the rest of the wolf pack and disappeared into the woods.

The gypsies murmured amongst themselves, "What kind of dog is this?" Should we trust this animal that can behave like a demon? Mark's father wept again and asked "What about my boy? King is our only chance. Let's give him time, at least until we get to the mountains."

The rest of the group talked it over and agreed to follow King until they reached the mountains. They had entered the forest once again and finally the mountains appeared seemingly at their feet. Their confidence in King had returned. He was gentle again, so they continued to follow him and Mark's father. They climbed way up the mountain. The first part was easy going because it was just little hills and loose rocks with grass running through the crevices between them. When the men stopped and looked around, they were very

high up. For a moment they enjoyed the beauty of the land that lay stretched out below them, but King let out a howl that got everyone's attention. They all looked in King's direction and their hearts leapt with joy, and big smiles spread across their faces.

Someone was lying below them on a rocky ledge. The men shouted and the echo of their voices awakened a young lad who stood up and shouted back to them. It was Mark. As they began to make their way toward him, they noticed a huge bear also heading for Mark from the other direction. The gypsies shouted to Mark to run from the bear, but it was too late. As Mark turned around the bear hit him on his shoulder, causing him to lose his balance and tumble over some rocks before sliding to a stop. He screamed as King dashed out, and sprang from the rocks above right over Mark, landing on the bear's back. This caused the gigantic animal to roll and tumble away from Mark. Then the bear shook its head and lunged toward King. King waited for just the right moment, and then sank his teeth into the bear's black nose. Then, as King let go of him, the bear quickly turned and ran off as fast as it could, to put as much distance between them as possible.

After his father treated Marks's wounds, the group made their journey back to camp. About a mile from their campsite, King went over to the father and son who were resting. His job was done, so he licked Mark's face and ran swiftly back into the woods. When the group of gypsies returned, everyone was so happy that they decided to have a great feast. Mark's father told everyone about the rescue and now wherever the gypsies go, they tell the amazing tale over and over again of how a wolf-dog named King had saved Mark's life.

# King and the Outlaws

A s the sun rose early one fall morning, the galloping of horses awakened the town folk. When they peeked out of their windows, they saw seven horses. Their riders were unshaven, mean looking men, in long black coats with their hats tipped to one side. As their coats blew backwards, the handles of their guns caught the early morning light. The town folk were a bit worried until they saw the shiny silver badges on the riders' chests.

As the men pulled up to the saloon, Arnold the town's Sheriff greeted them solemnly. The leader of the posse was sheriff Dalfe. He had a firm handshake, but the muscles in his face were tense. While the other deputies went into the saloon, the sheriff went with Arnold to his home. There they sat down on the porch to have coffee. Arnold asked the sheriff why he was in town, and the sheriff replied that he didn't want to alarm Arnold, but he was looking for three dangerous men who had escaped from prison. They were last seen heading towards the town and could be hiding in the nearby woods. Arnold offered to help in the search, but the sheriff insisted, "No one knows the woods better than me." The sheriff thanked Arnold however, saying, "We will rest today, but early tomorrow morning, be ready to ride." With a smile they shook hands again, and the lawman departed.

Deep in the forest, the three tired and hungry outlaws suddenly came upon Mr. Herbert's cabin in a clearing in the woods. They felt their empty stomachs jump with anticipation as they imagined warm food, drinks and maybe, just maybe, warm beds to sleep in. Without a sound, they crept around the cabin and looked in through the windows. They soon saw Mr. Herbert in his chair fast asleep. Dan, the leader, shouted, "Hey, there's only an old man inside!" They were all laughing as they knocked on the door – this was going to be too easy!

Mr. Herbert woke up with a start, who could that be knocking? Still half asleep, he opened the door. The three men pushed their way right past him, shouting, "OK, where's the food?" They went straight for the old man's kitchen cabinets. Anything that they could get into their mouths, they ate. Mr. Herbert shouted, "This is my home, not a pig pen!" but Dan told him to shut up and one of the other men hit Mr. Herbert hard on the head, knocking him unconscious. They tied him tightly to a chair and stuffed his mouth with a cloth, then continued to feast on his food. After having their fill, they all went outside and bathed in the stream, splashing water all over each other like little children. Freshly shaven, they came inside and helped themselves to Mr. Herbert's clothes. As they sat around the table drinking coffee and playing cards, the old man regained consciousness.

The day had passed quickly and when the stars came out one by one, they were still playing their card game. Suddenly Dan looked up and through the window saw eyes that were glowing red and angry like a demon's. Dan drew his gun and shot at the creature over the heads of his partners, who ducked under the table wondering what was wrong. Then Dan stood up, opened the door and went outside, but saw nothing. He came back inside and apologized, " I thought I saw the devil," he said. They all laughed it off and continued their game with fresh cups of coffee.

When the game was finally finished, one of the outlaws rose. " I'm going outside to take a look around." He loaded his gun and walked outside, breathing the crisp fresh air and enjoying his stroll

around the cabin. A noise coming from the old man's barn made him jump. Gun in hand, he slowly opened the barn door, which made a loud screech that scared the barn cat, causing it to give a long, loud hiss.

The outlaw screamed and fired a shot in the direction of the barn cat, nearly hitting him. He had to laugh at himself for being scared of a cat. He put his gun back in the holster and turned around to walk out, then froze – between him and the barn door stood King with fire in his eyes. Before the outlaw could reach for his gun, King leaped at his chest and knocked him to the ground. The man's head hit a large rock and he passed out.

The other two outlaws heard the commotion outside and both ran to the window and looked out. All they could see was that the barn door was partly open. Dan ordered the other man to go out and see what was going on. The man walked towards the barn with his gun in his hand.

Dan was watching from the window. He was astonished when he saw a shadow moving up slowly behind his friend. "Look out!" he shouted. The outlaw turned just as King leapt on him, well before the man had a chance to react. In shock and fear, the outlaw keeled over in a faint. Through the window Dan began shooting at the pair, not caring if he hit friend or foe. He took the rag out of Mr. Herbert's mouth and shouted, "What's out there?" The old man gasped for air and said, " If I were you I would leave now, because that thing out there is coming in here for you next." Dan said, " Shut up, you're in no position to threaten me. If I die, you die first." And he held the gun to the old man's head. "Any last words before you meet your maker?" Mr. Herbert looked up at the outlaw and smiled, "I'll see you, when you get there."

At that, King burst through the window. Dan fired a single shot but missed. King leaped on Dan and knocked the gun right out of his hand. Although Dan badly wanted to make a run for the gun that had landed nearby at Mr. Herbert's feet, King's growl kept Dan frozen to the floor in fear.

Meanwhile, King's sharp teeth gnawed through the rope that bound Mr. Herbert until he was completely free. While King stood guard, Mr. Herbert tied Dan up. Then King lead Mr. Herbert to the

other outlaws. Mr. Herbert wasted no time tying them up too. And, although Dan was very heavy, he even managed to drag him outside and put him with his pals.

Back in town, Arnold saddled up early with the sheriff and his deputies. They searched everywhere. They found no sign of anything or anyone until they came to Mr. Herbert's log cabin. There, in the middle of the yard, were the three outlaws dressed up like Christmas turkeys. King rushed out of the cabin growling. As one, they all reached for their guns, but Arnold shouted, " Put your weapons down. That's King. He lives with the old man." Arnold walked up to King, bent down and patted him gently, while King wagged his tail in a friendly manner, but the dog still kept his eyes fixed on the strangers who had slid their guns back into their holsters again. Just then, Mr. Herbert appeared at the cabin door with his rifle in his hand and greeted Arnold, who explained who the men were and why they had come. Mr. Herbert invited them all indoors, made coffee and told them what happened and how King had saved his life.

They stayed quite a while, listening to the old man's stories about King, their eyes wide with amazement. Finally, they said their goodbyes and took the outlaws back to town. After their long journey back to the prison, the deputies told everyone about the wonder dog named King, and how he had helped them capture the outlaws.

# The Government Agents

Stories of King continued to spread across the country. In addition, Mr. Herbert was gaining the reputation as the best dog trainer in the land. News of their adventures did not go unnoticed by the army, and even reached the ears of General Phillips at the base in St. Thomas, where Mr. Herbert was stationed when he was in the army.

Out of curiosity, General Phillips looked up Mr. Herbert's record and learned that he had been discharged from the army several years earlier, after receiving an injury. It was an injury to his head that had put him in a coma for a week, and when he did regain consciousness, he was never quite the same. General Phillips turned the page and found a letter attached to Mr. Herbert's file. It said that two weeks after Mr. Herbert's discharge, one of the army's Alsatian puppies, that was no more than eight months old, went missing. Her name was Lady. Everyone suspected Mr. Herbert, because he spent more time training Lady than any of the other army dogs.

General Phillips smiled to himself. If this was the same Mr. Herbert, what a neat thing it would be for the army to claim back its property. Since King was the offspring of Lady, he really belonged to the army as well. He called in two of his most trusted agents Sack and Muster and showed them the records. He told them that he wanted them to go to Pier's Town to find Sheriff Dalfe. Dalfe would know how to find Mr. Herbert. He gave them a letter with a government stamp and told them, "If you have any trouble, give him this letter." Before they left, General Phillips said, "By the way, I would like this dog named King kept alive and well."

When the agents reached Pier's Town, they introduced themselves to Sheriff Dalfe who invited them into his office. He offered them coffee and while they were sipping it, Sheriff Dalfe said, " So, tell me what brings you here to visit me?" Sack said, "We have heard of how you helped in capturing the three prison escapees and…" The sheriff interrupted, "Not me. I didn't do anything." Sack said, "We know that Sheriff. We are interested in the dog called King." " In what way are you interested in a dog?" asked the Sheriff. "Well, you see King and his mother really belong to the army," Sack replied. "But, how is that possible?" Dalfe asked. Sack handed him the letter. After Dalfe read it, he asked, "And just what must I do to help the army?" Muster answered, " Your job is simple. Take us to the old man and we will do the rest." Then Sack rose from his seat saying, "We will be ready to ride first thing in the morning." Alone in his office again, after they had left, Sheriff Dalfe grumbled to himself. He was not looking forward to tomorrow, not one little bit.

The next morning it was raining, making the day cold, damp and the road very muddy. A wagon drawn by two horses and carrying the Agents went ahead of Sheriff Dalfe, who rode along on his own horse behind them. As they rumbled along, the wagon wheels kept spitting mud up into Dalfe's face, which didn't improve his mood at all.

When they got to Fiddler's Town, they stopped for supplies and to rest their horses and themselves. Arnold was surprised to see Sheriff Dalfe back again and welcomed him to spend the night at his home. After settling in, Sheriff Dalfe showed Arnold the letter. "I want to go and warn Mr. Herbert," Arnold said. Sheriff Dalfe reminded him that he would be breaking the law if he stepped in. "I would be forced to arrest you," he said. So Arnold promised not to make any trouble. His last words to the sheriff before retiring to bed were, "Now I know how a tree feels when all its leaves are blown off and it stands there naked through the cold winter."

The sheriff lay in his bed staring out of the window at the bright stars that shone over the wilderness. His gaze was thoughtful, but after a time he too fell asleep.

The next morning soft raindrops made a musical tapping sound on the window and woke Sheriff Dalfe. He thought about the first day he became a sheriff. He was nervous dealing with people, because he wanted to please everyone. He soon learned that the law had to be obeyed and, if broken, the consequence was always a punishment of some kind. He was pulled back from his day-dreaming when he heard a loud knock on Arnold's front door. "Your friends are here Sheriff" Arnold shouted out. The sheriff quickly dressed and came down to say goodbye to Arnold, who asked him if he was sure he remembered the way. Sheriff Dalfe smiled, he said once he had been to a place, he never forgot how to find it again.

The day was very wet again, causing them to stop many times to pull the wagon wheels out of the cement-like mud. When they finally reached the road that cut toward the east, they had to travel through some thick woods. A small rocky path led deep into the area. The thick trees and tall pines allowed only enough room for one wagon to travel with the Sheriff still behind on horseback. About three miles into the woods, the group came to a clearing and there stood Mr. Herbert's cabin, with a small barn to the east of the house. During the summer, it would be almost completely hidden by fields of corn.

As they rode up to the cabin, a light snow began to fall. They could see the barn clearly and the partly open door. Dalfe got off his horse and started walking toward the barn. Muster shouted, "Sheriff, your job is finished, so don't you utter a single word to the old man about our purpose here"

Dalfe glanced over his shoulder and replied, "I hear you sir, loud and clear." When the sheriff entered the barn, Mr. Herbert was sitting on a stool cleaning the thick mud from his boots. He raised his head and saw the Sheriff standing over him. With a smile he said,"Hi Sheriff. What brings you here? Don't tell me you have another escapee!"

The sheriff smiled. "No, I'm just passing through. I've got two government agents with me. I'm on a private mission and we just stopped to avoid the snow. We hoped that we could enjoy a cup of coffee and your friendly hospitality." Mr. Herbert told Dalfe to go inside and he would join them as soon as he finished his boots. The sheriff and the agents entered the cabin and made themselves comfortable. The snowfall grew heavier outside. Dalfe gazed out of the window. "We might have to spend the night. I'll go put the horses in the barn." Mr. Herbert was just returning from the barn so he helped Sheriff Dalfe until the horses were comfortably settled. Then they all gathered inside the cabin in the glow of the log fire.

Dalfe introduced the agents to Mr. Herbert, who was really happy to have company. Right away he began telling stories about King. Some of the stories were so amazing that the agents shook their heads in disbelief. Mr. Herbert continued, but Muster interrupted. "Where is this wonder dog, King now?" " Somewhere out there in the woods helping anyone or any animal in trouble", said Mr. Herbert. King has no special time to be home – his home is out there." Then Muster asked, "What is this King, a wild dog?" "No," said Mr. Herbert, "King just has a mind of his own and is highly intelligent, so I will not keep him in captivity."

Muster laughed it off and said that he would like to see this dog called King for himself. And, until he did, King was just something from their imagination. Mr. Herbert's feelings were hurt, but he hid it. Muster got up from his seat to get another cup of coffee. On his way back, he looked out the window. Eyes of fire were staring straight into his. Muster dropped his cup and shouted, "What's that?" Mr. Herbert smiled "That's King." He let the dog in. King shook

himself and flakes of snow scattered all over the rug.

Muster and Sack hid behind Dalfe and pleaded with Mr. Herbert to take the wolf dog out. They stared at the animal in fear. Mr. Herbert said. "Fear not," as King walked over and lay down beside the fire. Muster nodded. "After seeing the size and build of that wolf dog, I am convinced all your stories are true."

As the day slowly passed and night fell, there were no stars to be seen shining through the heavy clouds leaving the woods looking much darker than normal. It was the perfect night to be inside the cabin close to a welcoming fire. Mr. Herbert made a delicious cream of corn soup that warmed right through their chilled bodies. Muster himself went over to give King the last portion of soup. No one, not even Sack, saw Muster sprinkle some white powder into King's soup. King wasted no time and gobbled the soup down. Then he lay next to the fire and fell right off to sleep.

When the agents were sure that King was sleeping, they told Mr. Herbert their purpose. They showed him the letter. After reading it, Mr. Herbert said, "Please leave, all of you. You are not welcome here." He reached for his rifle, but Muster gripped Mr. Herbert's arm and pushed him aside, making him fall to the floor.

Sheriff Dalfe raced to Mr. Herbert's side and helped him up. He shouted at the agent. "This is not necessary, Muster!" Muster pointed the rifle at the sheriff and said, "Dalfe, I told you your job is done. Not another word from you!" Mr. Herbert fought hard to break free from Dalfe and in the ensuing struggle, his heart stopped and he collapsed in Dalfe's arms and died. Dalfe cried out loud, " Now look what you have done."

Muster stalked over to Dalfe and hit him with the rifle butt across his head. King slept through everything. Sack and Muster tied King's legs and mouth, making him helpless. They tied the sheriff to a chair. Sack asked, "What are we going to do with the old man's body?" "There is nothing we can do for him," Muster replied, "Take the body outside." So they dragged his lifeless old body outside and left it alone in the cold.

By morning, the snow had stopped. Dalfe, who was still trying to break free, awakened the agents with all his struggling. Now he had fallen to the floor while still tied to the chair. Muster went to the barn and got the horse and wagon ready to go. He passed the old man's

body and noticed it was partly frozen and his beard had small pieces of ice hanging from it. When Muster got back to the cabin, he helped Sack drag King out. King was still fast asleep, and with difficulty they managed to put the huge creature on the wagon. They went back in and put a little of their white powder herb in some water and held Dalfe's head back forcing it down his throat. In a few minutes he was asleep too. Sack untied him and Dalfe fell at their feet. Then Muster joined Sack leaving Dalfe behind.

Sack had the reins in his hands which he flicked to set the horses off galloping. Muster sat beside him looking back at King lying helpless and asleep. The old man's cabin disappeared behind them and only tall pines surrounded them as they traveled swiftly along the rocky path. They rode over a bump that jostled the wagon so violently, that Muster almost fell out. He gripped the seat tightly and when he looked back, he saw that King had awakened. His eyes were open and tears were running down his cheeks. Muster laughed. "Look Sack, the great King is crying."

King tried to open his mighty jaws but the rope held them shut. After many attempts, King stretched the rope some more giving his teeth enough room to gnaw the rope through and free his mouth. King let out a howl so loud it frightened the horses who had to be pulled to a halt. Muster was so terrified that he reached for his gun and pointed it at King, who lay there with his legs tied. Sack shouted, "Don't shoot! This dog is my retirement!"

Muster put his gun back and said, "I don't know how he managed to get his mouth free. His teeth must be as sharp as a razor to cut that rope." Sack started the horses again. Birds gathered and flew over the wagon as it rode along, as if they were interested to see where the helpless cry was coming from.

Muster pointed. "What is that?" Sack pulled the horses to a

stop. About seventy-five yards up the path stood King's father, Big Gray, and by his side stood Lady. Muster lifted his gun and fired over the horses' heads at the wolf and the Alsatian. The horses stamped, snorted and tried to turn around. They yanked the wagon into the thick pines until it was stuck. Big Gray and Lady ran back into the woods. Sack shouted, "What are you doing, Muster? Put the gun away and help me get these horses out of the bushes!"

They finally freed both the horses and the wagon and before they knew it they were back on their journey. They still had about a mile left before they came out of the rocky woods. King wriggled tirelessly to free himself.

Several howls rang out and a very nervous Muster reached for his gun. He looked around with one hand on his gun and the other holding onto the wagon. He glanced over his shoulder to look back at King and was shocked into panic when he saw the biggest pack of wolves he had ever seen following behind the wagon. He could not see the end of them. Muster's heart felt as though it was in his mouth. Speechless, he went limp and the next bump sent Muster tumbling into the back of the wagon right next to King. He jumped to his feet, only to lose his balance once more. This time Muster fell and one of his feet got wedged between two boards at the rear of the wagon. As they raced down the trail it was only Muster's trapped foot that kept him from falling off.

Sack saw the pack of wolves and was afraid to stop, even though Muster was being dragged off the back and was screaming for help. The wolves drew closer. They were about twenty-five yards from Muster, when his foot slipped out of his boot, causing him to tumble onto the muddy ground. The wolves wasted no time, swarming over Muster and tearing him to shreds. Up ahead, about a hundred yards away, a clearing appeared through the trees that brought a smile to

Sack's face, but the horses shied again and again and tried to turn back into the woods. Then the wagon tumbled over sending King and Sack flying through the air, side by side onto the ground.

King had managed to chew through the ropes that were tied to his front legs, but his back legs were still tied. Sack rose to his feet and saw Big Gray and Lady in front of him. He understood why the horses had tried to run away. Sack reached for his gun, but the pack of wolves caught up to him and knocked him down and the gun from his hands before he could fire. Big Gray and Lady watched as the pack

tore into Sack. When it was over, Sack lay dead.

All the wolves now gathered around King who lay still as a statue. Big Gray stood over King and howled. Lady walked over and gnawed through the rope on his hind legs with her sharp teeth. King tried to stand, but fell back to the ground, his legs still weak and numb from lack of blood circulation.

Big Gray licked the places where the rope had been tied to King, helping the blood to flow. After a while, King stood and all the wolves howled. He looked around, then howled a mighty howl of respect and appreciation. Big Gray and Lady, with King between them, ran into the woods and led the pack east into the mountains. The whole woods echoed with wolf howls as if a new leader had been crowned.

When Sheriff Dalfe regained consciousness, he dug a deep grave and solemnly buried Mr. Herbert next to the Post where the bell that he always rang to call King to come home hung. After a short prayer, Dalfe left. Along the track he found the remains of Muster and Sack, so he stopped and took them back to St. Thomas and gave them into the care of General Phillips.

# Wolfgang

Two years passed after the death of Mr. Herbert. Arnold was still the town sheriff and King was the new leader of the wolf pack since the death of Big Gray a year earlier. The big wolf had become caught in a trap that belonged to Wolfgang, a trapper who made his living selling hides and skins.

Arnold warned Wolfgang many times not to set traps near his town. "I'll destroy every trap that I find," threatened Arnold. "If I catch you doing that I will not hesitate to shoot you,' warned Wolfgang. His threats never stopped Arnold, until one spring morning, Wolfgang caught Arnold destroying one of his traps. Arnold turned around to find that he was looking down the nose of a rifle. Wolfgang yelled, "I warned you!" and he kicked him. Arnold tumbled back and Wolfgang took aim.

A harsh voice rang out from behind him. "Drop that rifle, or I'll blow you to kingdom come!" Wolfgang dropped the weapon and slowly turned to look into the eyes of a scruffy man. His face was covered with a heavy beard. Wolfgang pleaded, "Stranger, I have no fight with you. I was only trying to scare Arnold. We are really friends." He reached out a hand to help Arnold up, but Arnold slapped his arm away and climbed to his feet on his own." I thank you. If you had not come when you did, this animal killer might have

murdered me."

The bearded man still had his rifle pointing at Wolfgang. "Do you want me to shoot him?" Wolfgang dropped to his knees and pleaded with Arnold to tell the stranger not to shoot. Arnold looked into the stranger's eyes and knew the man would shoot Wolfgang without a second thought. "Wolfgang, if I tell this stranger not to shoot you, would you leave this town and never trap an animal again?" "I will, I promise," he replied.

Arnold said to the stranger, "Don't shoot him, I think he has learned his lesson." Turning to Wolfgang, he shouted, "Now get far away from here. I never want to lay eyes on you again." Wolfgang wasted no time, he ran off, leaving his rifle on the ground.

Arnold reached out. "Thank you stranger. My name is Arnold, I'm the town Sheriff." The stranger smiled, "I know. I'm sheriff Dalfe. You didn't recognize me." Arnold let out a cry of joy as both men embraced. "What happened to you?" Arnold asked. "You look as if you haven't shaved for years." Arnold invited Dalfe to his home, where Dalfe bathed and shaved. After a hot meal, they both went out to sit on the porch

Dalfe said, "I guess you are wondering why I am here." Arnold nodded, "I knew you would get around to telling me when you were ready. So, what brings you here, man business or wolf business?" "Neither," said Dalfe. "I'm no longer working. The army thought I had something to do with the death of Sack and Muster, but could not prove anything. However, some high-ranking people managed to influence my superiors, and I lost my job. I've been drifting from town to town for more than a year."

"But what brought you here?" "I'm not getting any younger," said Dalfe. "I was thinking about settling down, if I could find a piece of land." Arnold smiled. "Old man Herbert's land is up for sale. With a little work, the cabin could be restored to living condition; if you want, we can start first thing in the morning." "Then we better get some sleep." Dalfe said.

The next day they loaded their wagon with tools and food and left town. When they reached the rocky path that led to the cabin, they had to get out of the wagon to remove all the broken branches that blocked the path. After about three miles, they could see the cabin in the distance. It was covered with vines. As they came nearer, they could see the barn next to a cornfield overgrown with weeds too. The men went right to work. At the end of the day, the cabin was clean and livable again.

Within two weeks, the cabin was completely repaired and the barn was ready to be filled with animals. The fields had been plowed and were ready for planting. Even the old bell on the wooden post next to the well had been polished.

In the fall, Dalfe harvested his first crop of corn. He stored some and took the rest to town to sell. Arnold was his first customer. After Dalfe sold all his corn, he joined Arnold for a coffee. Arnold asked, "So tell me, Dalfe, have you seen him?" "Who?" asked Dalfe. "King," Arnold said with a smile. "No, but I hear howls throughout the night. I don't think King could ever be friends with men again." Dalfe rose. "I'd better be leaving, I've got animals to feed."

Dalfe stocked up with food and supplies before leaving town. When he reached home, he was greeted with a loud squeal, as if an animal was in some kind of pain. Dalfe jumped from the wagon. The noise seemed to be coming from the well. He ran over to the well and instead of a bucket at the end of the rope, one of the pigs was there, screaming for its life. Dalfe pulled him up and unwrapped the rope from his neck. The poor pig gasped for breath. Dalfe gently rubbed his neck until the pig stopped squealing. Dalfe nearly fell over when he heard a sly voice behind him say, "Poor little pig, somebody must have tried to hang him."

Dalfe spun around to find himself looking down the barrel of Wolfgang's rifle. Dalfe said, "I knew that I should have shot you." Wolfgang shook his head, "You're not so big without your gun. You made me look like a fool. Now it's your turn to look like a fool. There's no one around for miles to hear you scream." He fired a shot at Dalfe's feet. Dalfe jumped back and hit the wooden bell post and the bell made a loud ding-dong that echoed throughout the forest. "Not just yet though!" Wolfgang lifted his rifle. "I want to see you suffer first." He fired a few more shots that missed Dalfe by inches.

Then Wolfgang laughed and said, "Goodbye." Slowly he raised his gun and pointed the barrel at Dalfe's head.

Before he could pull the trigger, he heard a slight noise behind him and turned to find King in midair. The wolf dog leapt upon Wolfgang and Dalfe grabbed Wolfgang's gun from him. Now he and King were in control. He wasted no time tying Wolfgang up, so he could take him back to town and put him behind bars. He turned around to thank King, but the wolf dog was gone.

The next evening it was raining. The thunder roared, the lightning flashed and the wind whistled eerily through the trees. Dalfe sat in his cabin watching the lightning turn night into day with every flash, it was so bright. Inside, he felt safe and dry with the blazing fire to keep him warm. But he did feel lonely, and wished Arnold was still there working with him. Outside he heard a loud howl. He looked out the window and watched as a shadowy figure moved out of the forest and headed towards the cabin. At first he was worried, but then he realised it was King carrying something that looked like a small animal in his mouth. The wolf dog ran up to the door and placed something gently on the step before turning and heading swiftly back the way he had come.

Dalfe threw open the cabin door, lifted the little creature and carried him gently inside. He dried him carefully with a soft towel and laid him down close to the warmth of the fire. Then, as he watched the puppy curl up on the rug, a big smile spread slowly across Dalfe's face. "Imagine that," he said quietly to the sleeping puppy. "Just as years ago Lady left King as a puppy for Mr. Herbert, now King has returned and left you as a companion for me."

www.ingramcontent.com/pod-product-compliance
Lightning Source LLC
Chambersburg PA
CBHW061504170626
46811CB00004B/1602